THE CITY OF LIGHT

A
CHRONICLES OF THE DERGO KNIGHTS
QUICK READ

REBECCA HILLARY

ISBN: 978-1-326-21326-8

Chronicles of the Dergo Knights

A trilogy of fantasy novels set in the kingdom and city of Beranonir.

The Chronicles follow the fortunes of several characters:

- Hendrik, a young man joining the Order of the Knights of Dergo, who holds a potentially life-changing secret.
- Shan, Hendrik's sister and future Queen of Beranonir, whose only wish is for a normal life.
- Sir Aiden, a Dergo Knight whose destiny intertwines with those of Hendrik and Shan when he accompanies them on their journey to the royal city of Beranonir.
- Lord Borain, the lost Dergo Knight whose return foretells of the death of the king.

King Rhidian, the King of Beranonir whose time appears to be growing short.

Chapter 1

In the days before the Third War, Toth was a peaceful city on the borders of the verdant valleys of the kingdom of Beranonir, in an area known as the Galonian Steppe. Barbarian raiders stalked the steppe however there were few attacks on Toth. The Duke's personal guard dealt with those that occurred swiftly and with a minimum of bloodshed, thus sparing the children of the city the horrors of battle. The green knights, so called because of the patina of their armour, were well trained and efficient in their slaying of the barbarians, and the city remained untouched by savagery.

When the stirrings of war began, the citizens of Toth cared little. They had grown accustomed to their place of safety on the steppe. For ten long years, the war reigned and cities fell to the enemy and with each passing moon, the people of Toth rejoiced that their city stood.

Then came the fall of the barbarian stronghold of R'nim. The barbarians took personal exception to the attack on their major city, and as Toth was the closest city, they held the people of Toth responsible. They cared not that Toth was incapable of raising an army, and so they began their assault, week after week, on the only untouched city in the kingdom.

The Green Knights fought valiantly against the barbarian raiders, cutting down each attack in mere hours, and the city stood, as strong as ever, against their assault. What the knights did not foresee was that the barbarians might amass an army against them. With every attack, their numbers grew until, after four months, whole battalions were at the gates of Toth.

The Duke called his advisors to him, a panic in his heart and a fear for the people of the city. They agreed that they must do something to stop the attacks, but how could they stop an army of unstoppable barbarian warriors? Envoys despatched to the royal city invariably returned across the back of their own horse, messenger birds seemingly never reached their destination, no doubt becoming food for the barbarian table.

"Something must be done." The Duke insisted, his seat at the head of of the table giving him full view of his advisors and they of him. "Never in its history has Toth been victim of such barbarity."

"What do you suggest we do?"

"Our cries for aid are going unheard."

"Beranonir has fallen, Your Grace. There is nothing more to be done."

"Beranonir has not fallen." The Duke snapped. "As long as the king lives, Beranonir will stand. He has his sons and they theirs. Beranonir will not fall to these heathens."

"And who is to say that the king lives, Sire?" The same

man spoke again. "We have had no word from Beranonir for almost a year. For all we know, the king could be dead and his children along with him. Toth may well be the last city remaining of this once great kingdom."

"Beranonir is the greatest kingdom!" The Duke roared. "Who are you to question the might of tis king, this city and this realm?"

"I am Drath, Sire. Your military advisor."

"I have had no need for a military advisor, boy. Who hired you?"

"Your wife, Sire." Drath replied, trying with all his might not to smirk.

"Yes, well I shall be having words with my wife at her earliest convenience. She has no right to appoint advisors without my approval." The Duke said. "So what say you, Drath? Would you not like to share your ideas with the rest of the room?"

"As I see it, our only course of action is to lay low, Sire." Drath got to his feet and strode around the table. "Perhaps train the more able men of the city to fight. A sort of militia if you will, but for the most part we will do nothing."

"Are you insane, boy?" The Duke gasped. "Your suggestion is that we allow ourselves to become lambs for the slaughter?"

"Insane? Perhaps. Lambs for the slaughter, hardly." Drath explained. "How many braziers would you say this city has?"

"Enough to light the city at night." Chirped the city ordinance adviser. "Enough to deter all but the most determined pickpockets and wastrels from plying their trade."

"And how many blacksmiths?" Drath asked. "How many men who could increase that number?"

"Three or four, I believe." The ordinance adviser mumbled. "Plus their apprentices. Several more men are more than capable."

"Then we have no time to lose. We must increase the number of braziers immediately. At least trebled, more if the materials will allow. The latest attack was yesterday, so I would hazard that we have a little less than a week for this to be done. Would that be enough time, Raith?"

"Perhaps, Sir." The ordinance adviser mused. "But what good would that do? Simply exhausting the city's supply of metal ore, which we should use for creating weapons, seems like a sorry waste of city resources."

"It will not be a waste." Drath turned to a tall and slender man at the end of the table. "My dear friend, Halkan. You are, are you not, the head of the Schymian council here in Toth?"

"I am." Halkan nodded. "As was my father before me. What does that have to do with your egregious waste of city resources?"

"Not a waste, my dear man." The young military

advisor grinned at him. "You are exactly the man we need if this plan is to work."

"Are you inclined ever to furnish us with this plan of yours, Drath?" The Duke interrupted. "You wish us to deplete our city's ore stock. You talk of the Schymian being the saviour of the city. You know as well as I that the Schymian cannot be trusted with such things. They have been the bane of this city since its founding."

"Forgive my impertinence, Sire, but if you hate the Schymians so heartily, then why do you have one amongst your closest advisors?"

"It is a tradition of the city that we have been unable to shake." The Duke scowled. "Tradition is what drives this city, and so the Schymian advisors remain."

The Schymian, Halkan, stared down at the table. He knew that his kind were not welcome. They had been outcasts in much of the kingdom for two centuries, and it was only in such remote cities as Toth that they still served a purpose. His life he spent apologising for the misdeeds of his forefathers, if misdeeds were what they were. Men were fearful of those born with magic. This was a fact known by many generations of Schymians. Their innate ability with the art of sorcery was both a blessing and a curse.

"Halkan, you should listen not to the ramblings of an old man in fear for his city." Drath told him. "He knows that you have your place. By the week's end, he will be on his knees, thanking you for your assistance in saving the city."

"Drath, I do not believe you need to be offering such promises." The Duke laughed wryly. "You will not change my mind about the Schymian. You come in here with your grand ideas and believe that they can undo decades of misery at the hands of these people."

"I not only believe them, I wholeheartedly guarantee it." Drath shrugged. "If you will not see reason then I feel sorry for you. Your hatred burns, and so too shall your city."

"Is that a threat?" The Duke roared. Every eye in the room turned to Drath, every man held his breath in anticipation of the young man's response.

"No, Your Grace, it is not a threat." Drath said confidently. "It is a promise."

Chapter 2

Drath walked through the streets of Toth with his hands in his pockets. It had been three days since the advisers had met in the palace, and three days since the Duke had laughed in his face. Fortunately, the Duke had been intrigued enough to allow Drath his way, and the blacksmiths were busy all across the city, forging braziers for his plan.

"Good morning, Willam." Drath announced cheerfully as he walked into the forge. "How goes your master on this fine morning?"

"Tired and overworked, sir." Young Willam replied. "What is your plan, if you do not mind me asking?"

"You will see." Drath winked. "Numbers, dear Willam. I need numbers."

"Fifty braziers completed so far, sir." Willam said. "And the same again by the week's end, I should not doubt."

"Very good." Drath smiled. "Very good indeed. I have no doubt that you and your master shall be well recompensed once my hunch is proven to be right."

"Whatever you say, sir." Willam shrugged and went back to his work. "I say this is fanciful, and we should be using the ore reserves to make weapons, but whatever you say."

"Keep up the good work, Willam." Drath tipped his hat.

"And give my regards to your master."

Willam nodded and Drath turned away into the street. He walked to the inn and slapped down two small gold coins onto the bar. "A mug of ale, if you please, my good man." He requested cheerfully.

"You are far too jolly for such an early hour." The barman grunted. "You keep the city awake night and day with the forge fires burning at all hours. It is a cruel and unusual man who would do such a thing, and no mistake."

"It will be worth it, mark my words." Drath assured him. "However you raise a good point. Perhaps some shutters should be made for the windows, so that your patrons will be enabled to sleep."

"My patrons care little for the eternal forge light." The barman shrugged, pushing a mug of ale towards the young man. "The more the forges burn, the more they drink. The more they drink, the more likely they will pass out."

"Then you could say that I am doing you a favour." Drath chuckled as he downed his ale.

"I readily admit that I have been making more money in the last days than usual. It seems rather odd since we have no new travellers staying at the inn. Those who were here are buying more ale, though, and that can only be a good thing."

"Then you are welcome." Drath laughed and pushed the empty mug toward the barman. "Now if you excuse me, I shall be on my way."

"Good morning to you, sir." The barman called after him as Drath walked out once more into the sunlight. He looked each way along the street and after a few moments' deliberation, turned left and walked toward the city gates.

"How goes it, sir?" The guard called down from the gate tower. "A fine morning it is today, would you not say?"

"A fine morning indeed!" Drath called back. "Any sign of the barbarians?"

"They have a camp set up beyond the horizon. That is all we know right now, sir. We send a horseman out twice a day, and none has suggested any movement so far."

"Will you let me know if there is any sign of movement?"

"Certainly, sir."

"How is that delightful daughter of yours? She must be approaching her age of betrothal, is she not?"

"That she is, sir. Just a few short weeks now, and nothing scares me more in the world. With a guard's dowry on offer, every man in the city with an eligible son is offering their name for consideration."

"Would it be impertinent of me to offer my own name?"

"You have a son?" The guard asked, confused. "You do not look old enough to have a grown son."

"Indeed I am not." Drath laughed. "I meant myself."

"My dear man, if this plan of yours pays off, I will marry you to Lansy myself!"

"Good to hear it!" Drath laughed. "Any chance of an

audience with the girl?"

"Certainly, sir! Go up to the house and tell, Marya, my wife that I sent you." The guard told him. "You know the way, I take it?"

"That I do." Drath nodded. "Good morning to you."

He turned and walked to the guard's house, a new spring in his step. He knocked brightly on the door and smiled openly to the young woman who opened the door. "Good morning, miss. Might I enquire if your younger sister is at home, and perhaps your mother?"

"They are both at home, sir." The girl curtsied. "Would you like to come in?" She held the door open and Drath walked inside. "They are in the drawing room."

Drath looked around the small house. It surprised him that such a small dwelling could be big enough to house a drawing room, and was not surprised when he was shown into a small room containing just a simple table, two chairs and a sparsely stocked bookshelf.

"Forgive my intrusion." He smiled as the guard's wife got to her feet. "Your husband said that I should come and visit."

"Yet another man with a son he wishes to marry off to my daughter, no doubt." The woman rolled her eyes. "Do we look as though he have a two gold pennies to rub together, much less this guard's dowry everyone seems so convinced we have on offer?"

"I no more have a son than you have a great wealth,

my lady." Drath held up his hand. "I have no need for another man's wealth. My family have endowed me with all the wealth I need."

"Then forgive my confusion, sir, but why are you here?"

"It is I who wish to marry your daughter." Drath nodded to the girl who looked at him shyly through a tangle of long, curly hair.

"You wish to marry my daughter, even though we do not have a dowry to offer?"

Drath leaned against the door frame and put his hands in his pockets again. "I am not getting any younger. I am almost twenty-five years old. I am becoming a laughing stock for the fact that I have not wed, and it is only a matter of time before the rumours will start that I favour men."

"Do you favour men?" The girl asked.

"You have a voice of your own?" Drath laughed. "I like that. I would not wish to take a wife who would not speak out for what she believes in."

"That is not the answer to the question I asked." The girl raised an eyebrow.

"No, it is not." Drath agreed. "No, I do not favour men. That is not to say that the rumours would be completely unfounded, but you would have no need to worry about my enthusiasm lacking in the marital bed."

"Praise be to Dergo for small mercies." The girl smiled and hung her head to hide the flushing of her cheeks.

"Such a forward daughter you have." Drath said to Marya. "So forward, in fact, that one would have to ask, is she still the innocent she appears to be?"

Lansy opened her mouth to speak, but found herself unable. She looked to her mother, who rushed to her side and put an arm around her shoulders. "Sir, forgive her. She is innocent, I assure you. However she has indeed known a man. He was older, and used his influence to sway her. He should not have done what she did, but some people cannot be persuaded to leave a young girl her childhood."

"How old was she?" Drath stood upright, incensed at the revelation.

"She was fourteen." Marya told him. "The first time."

"The first time?" Drath asked. "How long did this go on for?"

"Two years." Lansy sobbed. "He told me that my father would lose his position as guard of the gate. I did not wish to see my father on the streets, a pauper, at my doing. When he tired of me he cast me aside like a child casts aside a pup once it grows too old. He cut my father's wage as guard, and we are forced to live in this sorry state that you see."

"My dear girl, you are not to blame for this wrong that has been done to you. I will ensure that your family are well cared for, whether you accept my offer of marriage or not."

"That is very kind of you, sir." Lansy told him, wiping her eyes. "May I have until the week's end to give you my decision?"

"You may have as long as you need, dear one." Drath took her hands and laid a gentle kiss on her forehead. "It is my sincere hope that you say yes, but as I say, you may rest assured that I will make good on my promise to take care of your family in any case. Now, if you please, I will take my leave. I have much to do and little time to do it in."

As he walked from the room, leaving the women open-mouthed in shock, he dropped a purse of gold coins on the table, proving that he indeed was prepared to ensure their poverty would not continue.

Chapter 3

"The barbarians are preparing to move." The guard, Harin, rushed up to Drath on his daily visit to the gate. "Our scout returned not an hour ago and informed us that the barbarians will be on their way here by the end of the day."

"Then we have no time to lose." Darth clapped a hand down on Harin's shoulder. "You must gather as many of the Green Knights as you can to the gate. If the plan fails, I wish for as little damage to the city as you can manage."

"Yes, sir." Harin nodded. As Drath turned to leave, Harin caught his arm. "Thank you, for what you told my daughter. You seem to have turned her head, and that is no bad thing, but for you to offer to raise us from poverty is more than I could have hoped."

"I meant it, my dear fellow." Drath assured him. "I have no idea why you would not believe it."

"Oh, I do believe it, sir." Harin said. "Your generosity upon your leaving was also greatly appreciated. My eldest daughter has bought food and clothing and we are very much the better for it. My wife believes that I should stand above thanking you, but I could not allow such kindness to go unrecognised. You are in our prayers every night, and I pray that my daughter agrees to your offer of marriage."

"Harin, I pray for the same." Drath held the older

man's shoulder. "I know the horrific injustice that has befallen her, and I aim to put it right. Who knows how many other girls may have been treated in such a manner?"

"I wished that no man should ever know this of my daughter." Harin hung his head in shame. "You are a greater man than I for being able to accept my daughter even though she is no longer pure."

"Your daughter was not the one at fault." Drath corrected him. "She is an innocent girl who has suffered at the hands of a man who should have known better. His actions are despicable, and I will not rest until he is brought to justice for his crime."

"There is no crime, sir."

"Of course there is a crime. Do you honestly suggest that your daughter as complicit in his actions? Do you think that she acted as a willing participant? He threatened your family with destitution, and when he tired of her, he has left you in such a condition still. He is a vile and deplorable human being. If I did not care as I do for his wife, I would kill him myself and make it look like a barbarian assassination."

"Sir, I do not know what to say." Harin bowed his head to the younger man. "I now pray that Dergo in his wisdom brings you the greatest of fortune, and that he guides your hand in any way he sees fit."

Drath nodded and turned away, his heart pounding heavily in his chest. The braziers were still being fixed to the buildings of the city, and time was running short. The barbarian assault would come in hours and Drath still had to round up the Schymians in order for the plan to work.

He rushed to the house of Halkan, the Schymian from the meeting and pounded on the door. "Halkan, you are needed immediately, my friend." He gasped as he bent double from the run. "The braziers must be lit, as soon as you are able. I know we had hoped for more time, but it must be done now if we are to prevent the attack."

"By the powers of Dergo, this is sooner than I had thought." Halkan replied. "Are you sure?"

"It is imminent, Halkan." Drath ran a hand across his forehead, wiping away the sweat from his brow. "The scout says hours at the most. We must move now."

"Of course." Halkan nodded.

Between them, Halkan and Drath rounded up the Schymian sorcerers and posted them at intervals around the city. On Drath's mark, Halkan gave the order for the braziers to be lit. Within minutes, the city was ablaze. The fire danced and swam in the braziers, casting shadows across the city as it burned as brightly as the sun.

In the light of the braziers, shadows scattered as the city's people hurried to their homes, trying to reach the safety of their hearths before the attack that was known to be imminent. The news had travelled quickly, and so every man and woman knew that time was of the essence to get their children into their homes and secure every door and shutter.

Only one house remained open. The palace of the Duke was at the far end of the city from the gate and would be the last building to be attacked if the plan failed. Drath frowned at the thought of the Duke, sitting unthreatened in his drawing room, or making love to the duchess while outside in the city his people ran for cover. The Duke, by rights, should be cowering in the gutter. The attacks were of his making. Nobody had the nerve to say it, but it was due to the Duke's wasteful nature that the Green Knights were depleted in their numbers. The knights had been held in the highest regard for decades, second only to the king's own Royal Guard, but after the Duke had begun to divert funding from the training garrison, they began to decline in both number and discipline. The Duke had caused it with his irresponsible behaviour, his disregard for the people of the city, and a lack of compassion for the needs of others. He deserved to be in the streets with the Schymians who would save his city, not sitting comfortably in the palace.

"What now?" Halkan shouted over from his position by the gate. "What do we do now, my old friend?"

"Now we wait." Drath called back. "Hold your position, and do not drop your guard."

"Drath, my boy." Harin shouted down from the gate tower. "They have just broken the horizon."

Chapter 4

There was a deathly calm as they waited for the barbarian assault. The barbarian army marched ever closer, until they were within a distance that Drath could hear the sound of the war drums and the footfalls of their soldiers. By fortuitous circumstance, the sun set behind Toth, eclipsed by the city itself. Drath could almost hear the confusion of the barbarians as they beheld the burning city.

"What is happening, Harin?" He whispered up to the guard, his voice echoing around the silent plaza.

"They are sending forth a small raiding party." Harin whispered back. "What do you wish to do?"

"Hold steady." Drath instructed him. "Halkan, we need fireballs. Not big ones, but enough to make it seem as though the city is freshly burning."

"Not a problem." Halkan nodded, keeping one hand aimed at the braziers above him, he aimed his other hand toward the sky and sent a sparking ball of flame over the city wall. All across the city, the Schymians followed suit, with random fireballs flying in all directions.

There was a cacophony of screams as one ball of flickering flame flew low over the city gate and spun into the raiding party of barbarian soldiers. Drath saw Harin punch the air and could not help but to give a sigh of relief. The relief turned to dismay however, when Harin whispered down that the attack had not been stopped and that more barbarian soldiers were heading for the city. Drath thought for a few second, and then told Harin to open the gates, just enough that the barbarians would be able to enter the city, but not so much to indicate that the gates were only just opening.

"What are you thinking?" Halkan whispered. "This is suicide, Drath."

"Do you think I would risk the city?" Drath asked. "I am not going to let them take the city. Just wait."

"I hope you know what you are doing."

They waited as the footsteps of the barbarians approached the city gates, and within minutes there were a small number of them inside the city. The barbarians shaded their eyes against the blinding light of the magical fires in the braziers, but unable to see the militia men who now surrounded them. One by one, the barbarians were struck down, until only two remained.

"Burn them." Drath nodded in the direction of the barbarians and Halkan stared at him in disbelief.

"You want me to use my magic to kill?" Halkan was appalled. "I could never do such a thing."

"Just do it, Halkan." Drath told him.

Halkan shook his head, his face draining as he raised his hand toward the barbarian soldiers. The young men quivered with fear as they realised what was about to happen, and the fabric of their tunics began to smoulder. Halkan stretched out his fingers, closing his eyes to block out what he was doing, and the embers turned to flame. The young men yelped as the flames licked at their skin, but Drath crossed to the men and thrust them back out of the gate, barely concerned for himself as the flames danced about his arms. There was a roar from the barbarian army as they saw their two soldiers stumble out of the gate and fall in flames, writhing in agony.

"Why did you make me do that?" Halkan demanded. "There was no need for such a barbaric act. This makes us no better than they are."

"It was two men." Drath responded flatly. "Would you rather that army came in here and killed every man, woman and child in here? It was a diversionary tactic, Halkan. Go and join Harin on the tower if you do not believe that my intention was true."

Halkan stared at him and then hurried up the stone steps to the top of the tower. There he looked out at the barbarian army, which to his surprise was far smaller than he had anticipated. When the scouts had announced an army, he had expected a sea of soldiers as far as he could see. What he saw was around a hundred and fifty soldiers, far less than the total number of Green Knights and militia men in the city.

"What is the meaning of this?" Halkan asked the guard. "Why did the scouts say there was an army, when this is a ragtag bunch of soldiers at best?"

"This is an army, sir." Harin frowned. "I do not understand what you mean."

"This is not an army." Halkan laughed. "An army would stretch on over the horizon. An army would strike fear into the eye of its beholder. An army would be an awe-inspiring sight. This is just a rabble. This is not a fearful sight, Harin."

"This is indeed a fearful sight, sir." Harin insisted. It surprised Halkan to realise that the older man was serious. "This army would take this city in a heartbeat if we were not prepared in such a manner. Do you now feel less guilty for what Drath has made you do?"

"I certainly do." Halkan chuckled as turned to walk back down the steps.

"Wait, what is this?" Harin threw out his hand and grabbed Halkan's arm, turning him to look out onto the barbarian army. The army scattered in every direction as the Green Knights rode into their midst from the flanks. Within only a few minutes, the army was decimated, and only a handful of their number remained. The barbarian soldiers cowered in a small huddle as the Green Knights circled them. Halkan watched as the Duke rode his horse into the middle of the circling horses, his sneering voice audible even over their vast distance from the city.

"You have attacked my city for the last time." The Duke told them. "Beranonir stands, and you are defeated."

There was a sudden furore, and the Duke slumped forward on his horse. He fell to the ground where it became apparent that he was dead. The Green Knights despatched the last of the barbarian soldiers and rode with full strength back to the city.

"What happened?" Halkan shouted down to them. "What is the reason for the Duke's sudden demise?"

The commander of the Green Knights dismounted his horse and crossed to Drath. He bowed low to the young man and then knelt to kiss his hand. "Your Grace, your uncle is dead." The commander announced. "You are now the Duke of Toth. May the blessings of Dergo go with you."

Drath turned to the Schymian, his face impassive. "I know I should have told you, but this was the only way. My uncle was a cruel and brutal man whose waste has ruined this once great city. The city will be great once more." He announced to all those who would listen. "Let us rejoice in Toth's rebirth as the City of Light.

Lightning Source UK Ltd.
Milton Keynes UK
UKOW05f0423200117
292425UK00001B/206/P